Gaurav Mathur
A-802, Isle De Royale
ASF Insignia
Gwal Pahari
Gurgaon - 122003
91 7507503429
Gauravmathur027@gmail.com

BIOGRAPHY OF A NEW BORN

by Gaurav Mathur

Prologue

First child is the most exciting time for a couple in their lives. Anything that you try for the first time brings lot of joy and excitement and if this first time, is regarding bringing a new life in this world, makes you feel that you are the happiest couple around. The whole world revolves around the unborn. The food, travel, luxury, holidays, office and personal lives are adjusted to accommodate this sweet change.

As readers, we must have read about lot of parents penning down their thoughts and happiness and what all they must go through to bring this new life to earth. This is an attempt to think not as a parent, but a new life who is taking shape. This unborn shares his/her feeling and with utmost innocence describes the things happening.

I would like to thank my family and friends who helped me and my wife through this period and for all the wonderful advice and assistance during the 9 months period and beyond. Also, this biography may not have been possible without my beloved wife who shares every instance of her life with me and helped me in writing down all the experiences.

I also attribute it to the unforeseen circumstance experienced by my child when he was just 14 days old and had to go through a rarest surgery. But, the brave soul faced it and came out as the winner, bearing the scar of a warrior.

<u>Chapter 1: Discovery</u>

Knock, Knock! "Hey! Anybody there? Can anyone hear me?" cries the little one. *"I am here now. I am the one whom you were waiting for all these months. Hellllllooooo."* But, no one listens or reacts to the cries of the little fellow. And how can even listen or react to these calls, after all, this little fellow must not be more than a millimeter big. It has just entered this wonderful world and will require almost 9 months to be recognized and come out, much to the excitement of everyone around.

"Hmm, I believe I am too young or tiny to get noticed. Is this going to be the world for me? It is dark in here. Am I going to be safe? How am I going to survive, who will protect me?" The little hormone wondered. But then the realization sets in.

God had told that although you are a minuscule little hormone, but you are being planted in the womb of my own reflection called as 'mother'. No matter how tiny you are, knowingly and unknowingly, she is going to take care of you. She will be the one who will feed you. When you will grow a little big and trouble her, she will not mind and will happily tolerate all your devilish activities. For 9 months, she will protect you and will not make you feel afraid in the darkness of your current world. So, don't you worry about the current being. Just grow big and healthy and enjoy the pampering till you are inside and then a different pampering when you are outside.

"Ok! This sounds fun. I am going to be a good child and will not trouble mummy much, but some pampering will be required 😊*, let the time come."*

"2 weeks have passed, but no one is noticing me. I thought, everyone was waiting for me. Hmm, let me show some tantrums, " said the little fella. It is said that whatever activities take place inside the womb, they directly affect the mother. On 31st Oct 2017, the mother discovered that she has missed her monthly activity. There has been some feeling of nausea. It is better to do a home test and see if everything was ok. Father bought the pregnancy test kit and next morning, test was conducted.

"Here I am. Finally, you guys found it out." Both my parents were so happy and I did see couple of tears rolling down my mother's eyes and cheeks

in excitement. After all, that's what they were waiting for. So, there I was, giving an indication of my arrival. Straightaway, an appointment was fixed with the doctor. My father, a person who takes time to believe, wanted another home test to be done. Well, I cannot be a spoilsport and next morning, again I provided an indication of my presence. There was that 'test' line again, much more visible than the previous day.

I remember the dates as every day, my wannabe parents discuss about me at length.

On 1st Nov 2017, we visited the doctor. I was excited as I really wanted to understand how the next 9 months will be staged out, the precautions to be taken and the medicines that have to be taken to make me grow. So, we reached the hospital.

"Hello doctor", I said. Of course, I cannot be heard, but I wanted to be friendly as she will be the one who will bring me to this world. The doctor is a very nice and friendly lady. She has a very calm face and has years of experience in dealing with pregnancies. While we waited for our turn at the hospital, my father had done all kinds of research about the doctor. Apparently, she was the best Gynae around.

"Congratulations!" the doctor said after examining the photos of the home test. She also looked excited and we felt connected from the very first instance.

"Let me prescribe some tests and medicines. These tests are mandatory to determine the pregnancy and we need to ensure that all other

things like blood sugar, BP etc. are normal." The

doctor said while handing over the typed

prescription. It is dark and I am too young to

understand, but my mother read everything to my

comfort and I also read along with her. Let me look

at the tests:

1. Anti Rubella 1GG

2. Anti Rubella 1GM

3. CBC

4. FBS – Glucose

5. HBSAG

6. TSH – Thyroid Stimulating Hormone

7. VDRL (RPR/Syphilis)

8. Blood Group ABO & RH Gel Card

    Tchnique

9. Urine analysis

10. HB Electrophoresis (HPCL)

11. HIV

12. HCV

13. Total Beta HCG

14. USG Pregnancy early

"So many tests, OMG". I felt exhausted as I fumbled while reading the difficult names.

"We will get the tests done right now from the hospital", dad said in an exciting tone. He is a person who does not assume anything and bombarded the doctor with questions on what to eat, travel, rest and so on.

"She needs to eat home food, no outside food. Take rest and need not lift any weights." Dad was answered in a very calm mode.

Mom was scheduled to go for camping with her school kids. *"That's exciting".* I was thinking about it, but the doctor clearly said, *"no camping for you for now. It is going to be a hilly area, uneven surface and you may fall which will not be good for the baby. Since it is going to be a camp, even the doctor may not be easily available."* *"Please don't do this. I have seen mummy very excited about the camp. She has been running around making all the arrangements and ensuring there are no drop outs."* I was sad. But mom was cool. *"Agreed doctor. I will say no to camps, this is most important for me,"* mom pointed at her abdomen.

"No worries mummy, let me come out and then we all will go for lot of camping. I will be a rover."

I promised. Although, I cannot be heard, but somehow my parents understand my feelings from this stage itself and same words were reiterated by both. *"I am lucky to have such parents."*

We went to the laboratory for the tests. *"My goodness, this is such a big list of tests. You stupid nurse, you have taken 5 test tubes of blood from my mummy's body. She is already low on hemoglobin level and if you will draw out so much blood, won't she be weak?"* I was angry and upset that mom needs to go through all this. She also had to go through Ultrasound, which will tell how am I doing. *"Now, that's exciting. For the first time, I will be seen. Go ahead, determine me, find me. But, I am too small right now. Will I be noticed?"* I am naughty

I tried desperately to show my presence during the ultrasound. Right after the test, the doctor did confirm the presence, but informed that I am just about 2mm big. The test will not reveal anything, but the path is clear and the doctor does not see any blockages.

"Even if there were, I would have kicked them out", I was aggressive but then realized it is still time to develop my legs.

This news was enough, though, for my parents to start planning. The immediate discussion was around, how do we inform parents on both sides and my aunt. *"I am your special one, you better think of something nice, rather than the ordinary way of giving good news."* I demanded and to my eagerness, my parents did come up with a unique way. They created couple of images, one for my grandparents and one for my aunt. Although, one was very evident, the other one was tricky.

So, I am on the way of discovery to the immediate family as well.

"I am eager to see their faces. I am going to be naughty and let me see who are the ones I will be playing with most often."

In the afternoon, we reached home. We have a small window in my grandparents' room which opens on the side where we park our car. Since the time, mummy had sent the message, they were waiting and staring out of the window. We did not even ring the bell and they had opened the door. So eager to see my parents and hug them. I saw tears rolling down my grandma's cheeks. She hugged mom tightly and then there was that photo time.

Being a photoholic, mummy does not miss any

chance to click.

"Though I am tiny and do not feature in this photo,

I will start becoming evident in tests from now on".

I posed and posed and there we go, our first family

picture. *"Notice me! I am there tiny little person,*

2MM, with my mummy".

Rest of the day went in planning. Father decided to

change his shift to a morning one so that both my

parents can go together and come back together.

Such adjustment is wonderful to see.

Medicines were also purchased and mommy was

reminded to ensure that she eats healthy and takes

medicines on time in school too.

Chapter 2 – First Month (24th Sep to 23rd Oct 2017)

The first 3 months are said to be most crucial as this is the time most miscarriages take place.

"Mom, no jerks, no lifting of weights, no tiredness, proper rest, proper food, no junk food, no eating out and the list goes on." I was trying to remember all the instructions given to mom by my grandparents.

"No one knows of my existence other than the doctors and the small family". I wondered. *"But that's ok! Anyhow I cannot be pampered. Let me come out to this beautiful world and then I will be known to everyone. My cuteness will be unparalleled."*

Next phase was after 4 days – 4th Nov 2017, when we were supposed to collect the reports and meet the doctor. It was a Saturday. Though we will get the reports on Saturday, we got the doctor's appointment for Sunday. *"I can feel your eagerness.* I said to mom. She was very eager to see the reports and meet the doctor. It was a working day, but my parents went straight to the hospital to collect the reports. *"I am not a medical specialist, but the reports are easy to read". Hmm, RBC, these many. Good they fall under the bracket. Let me see, WBC, they are very good too. HCG, ha ha, cool,"*

We shared the reports with my grandparents too and then again, the crores of advices start coming. *"Well, I can publish a book now with Grandma's home remedies."*

It is important to get the opinion of the doctor at each stage, especially when tests are done. So, next day – on 5th Nov 2017, as per appointment, we met the doctor. I am 6MM now as per the new report and ultrasound.

"You can eat anything, but some of the factors need to be taken care of. Do not eat chilly and avoid oily food. Avoid food from outside as well to ensure proper hygiene is maintained. Avoid jerks." Doctor said after examining the reports. Mom had gone to the labor room and she was informed all this by the doctor. I can see my dad impatiently waiting outside as males are not allowed inside the labor room.

"It is hilarious to see dad like this". I said to myself. *"When no one can notice you, but you can*

notice everything is fun. I am enjoying this period of mine." I wondered as the doctor reiterated the same stuff to dad.

We came back home, planned everything and the whole family ensured that this is executed. Some standing instructions were:

1. Dad will pick and drop mom every day to avoid jerks. By the way, couple of months back we got a new car and I was really enjoying the rides of SUV.

2. Timely medication

3. One or two fruits a day

4. Half piece of Amla

5. Four almonds

6. Two cups of milk and;

7. Lots of laughter, rest and love

Things were going great. With each passing day, mom was looking beautiful. She has a flawless skin and free flowing hair. She carries herself very well and the effect of pregnancy were enhancing her beauty. Usual symptoms of my presence were felt like vomiting, slight back aches, slight head aches and mood swings. *"Dad is good in managing mom's mood swings."* I remember the incident when mom was cranky and getting angry for everything. A little kiss, funny jokes and pranks for half an hour by dad paid off and mom's mood swings were controlled.

But, who says, all good things do not have the other side. One day, mom went to the washroom for regular stuff and she noticed few drops of blood in the stool. That was worrisome. As soon as mom informed dad, I could see the worrying faces. My dad got up from the bed and immediately googled for the possible cause.

"I am fine dad, this must be some effect of medicines or constipation", it happens. *Please do not worry."* I was now worried by those looks on their faces.

During pregnancy, lot of muscle contraction takes place and it is normal for mothers to be constipated. Further, the effects of medicines also play its part. There can be some side effects of medicines too. Lack of intake of water, improper sleep, irregular timings for visiting loo and others can be contributing factors for constipation. It is also important to note from where the blood came out from the body.

Irrespective of the time taken, all these things were checked by my parents.

"This may be since I am constipated. Let us not worry. I am taking all precautions and this should not be critical at this point." Mom said to dad to calm him down. They researched further and realized the same after reading various articles. Our doctor had asked us to refer to the website – www.babycenter.com. This website contains all the details regarding each stage during pregnancy. It tells you what to eat, what to do in each month and precautions to be taken. After many reviews, they were contended and spoke about various precautions. Then the usual day went on.

"Phew! That was concerning. I know I am fine, but I can't express. Hope these 9 months go pass

quickly and I start expressing myself. Mom, dad start experiencing me". I was gloomy. *"What should I do now to make them happy?"* Grow big and healthy. I remembered those words. Mom is a glimpse of God and she will take care and she will be fine too.

CHAPTER 3 – SECOND MONTH (24th Oct to 23rd Nov 2017)

Second month is very exciting as the heart begins to form. Usual feeling of nausea, back ache, tiredness and mood swings continue. Doctor had advised that mom should get the ultrasound after 10-15 days. The usual precautions were to follow.

"It is such a lovely drive to mom's office, early in the morning". I used to love the fresh air and empty roads in the morning. As mom works as a Student Counselor, she is ought to be an enduring and stable person, so I am always relaxed. Timings of both my parents were matching so well and as a result of having offices close to each other, a short drive by mom from dad's office to and from was

not tiring, when he was having some early meetings.

The time was going very well. One week had passed since we had met the doctor. Mom took an appointment with the doctor for 19th Nov 2017. We got an early appointment and planned to get the ultrasound done post confirmation from the doctor. Before and after every test, it is advisable to consult the doctor so that proper advise can be obtained. So, on 19th Nov 2017, we were at the doctor's clinic, right on time. This additional responsibility had made mom very punctual. As I have heard dad saying that if we need to plan any outing, we should tell mom to get ready couple of hours in advance. Then, you can certainly hope to leave on time.

"I do not know whose genes I will get, but I would not mind sleeping that little extra." As we were waiting for our turn at the doctor's clinic, I knew what would be the result. *"I am growing and today everyone will hear the life inside me."* There were 4 ladies before us and all of them were in different stages of pregnancy. *"I wonder how mom will look when I will become healthier."* I was in my own thoughts when we were called in. After usual greetings, doctor examined the previous reports and asked us to get the ultrasound done.

We went to the hospital straight from the clinic. While mom was waiting, dad got all the formalities done and paid for the ultrasound. *"I am excited to see how the reactions will be."*

Mom was a little anxious as they did not know what will be the result. On our turn, both of us (I and mom) went inside. The doctor patiently examined and did the ultrasound.

"Guess what! There was it. Dig dig dig dig dig dig dig dig. 154 times a minute" Mom heard it and she could not stop smiling. Her immediate reaction was if dad can be allowed inside to hear this. The doctor agreed. Dad came in, a little nervous as no one had told why he has been called inside. Doctor showed him on-screen the little movement I was making. After all, this is the first time my parent will see me. *"11.2mm, dad. I have grown double in 2 weeks. Isn't it a decent progress?"* Then the doctor turned the instrument's volume to the highest and played the heartbeat.

DIG DIG DIG DIG DIG DIG DIG DIG DIG DIG DIG DIG

It was loud and clear. Dad smiled. I could see him that he is trying to control his smile. Trying to be mature, he controlled his smile and thanked the doctor for this gesture. *"thank you, doctor,"* I also said. I always feel happy to see my parents happy. We came out smiling and it was so uncontrolled that people waiting in the waiting area started looking at us. Mom felt shy but why? Their precious little munchkin is breathing life.

We went to see the doctor. Fortunately, our consultant was there as she was called for a delivery. She looked at the ultrasound report and congratulated us once again. *"Congratulations! Now, this will require you to take more precautions.*

You are having the best medicines available, so continue to take these until we do further tests. See you after 2 weeks." Our calm and capable doctor said to mom. Happy as we were, with smiles on our faces, we came down to the chemist and purchased the medicines. While dad was paying, mom informed parents on both sides as well as my aunt. *"There come more advices. I have stopped counting now as they are countless".* I felt exhausted at listening to all the same stuff again, but nice to see everyone's passion.

CHAPTER 4 – THIRD MONTH (24th Nov to 23rd Dec 2017)

From 24th Nov 2017, the third month had started. As important as in previous months, the diet plays a very important role. *"Mom needs to have 300 calories extra every day".* I read it in the website along with her. *"Hmm, some lovely sweet stuff, I guess. How about chocolates, candies, ice creams?"* My mouth would have become watery had I been a fully-grown baby, but still I wanted mom to eat all the delicious stuff. Being a non-vegetarian, I can expect lots of chicken, fish, mutton and what not. *"Yes mom, go for it. I will support you".* Despite being so tiny (11.2MM), I cannot stop expressing my feelings. Mom has been asked to follow the diet plan which advises that she eats 6-7 times a day:

- Corn Flakes in the morning when she gets up to reduce the effects of morning sickness

- A glass full off milk with a nutritional drink – lots of them are available in the market

- Bread with butter or Poha in the breakfast

- Some fruits with juices at around 12PM

- Healthy lunch thereafter

- A glass full of milk again with a nutritional drink in the evening or coconut water

- Light dinner

"Phew, that's a lot! But, I guess, that is required too as I will need these supplements as I grow in the months to come".

We came back home on 24th Nov 2017 from office and finally it happened. The first vomit during pregnancy. *"Mom is funny. She locks her inside the bathroom when she vomits so no one can see her"*. I smiled looking at her and wondering that she will be really angry at me if I smile or laugh at her on such a condition of hers in the future. Dad tried to help her, but he was asked to go out as she doesn't want anyone nearby. It is not a very good argument to have as in such conditions, women may feel weak and need support, but with mom, she is a resolute woman. I remember the conversation she was having with the doctor during our last visit that she feels nausea, but doesn't vomit. Doctor said that it is good, but it will happen eventually, as if the doctor knew the precise date and time.

"Ha ha ha! I thought people complain that they are vomiting, however during pregnancy, it is a reverse situation. Mom's want to vomit".

So, now the time has come to inform everyone. Whosoever called, mom, dad, grandpa, grandma kept informing. Same stuff was taking place at my grandpa's home (from mother's side) as they were so excited and informed all their relatives too. Being the child of a loving parent, as both my mom and dad were very loveable in the entire extended family, friends and relatives, the wishes start to pour in. WhatsApp was bombarded with messages and wishes. Although, the date was not confirmed by the doctor, but we assumed when the 9 months will be finished and told everyone that it's going to be the first week of July 2018.

In the month of December, lots of visits are planned and I am very excited about those. I want to meet everyone, personally. Although, I may go unnoticed, but I really want to see and meet everyone whom I am going to be playing with, enjoying and grow older. There is a grand reunion taking place at Udaipur where whole family and relatives will meet – around 50. All of us are excited about it and plans have been made for over a month now.

Days passed by and the whole week passed by performing the regular duties at office. As I am always with mom, I am learning a lot from her. The way she manages difficult children, it is pleasing to watch. *"I do not want to be a difficult child like these. Look at their parents, they look so innocent, but don't know how mischievous their children are.*

Anyhow, I hope, I can see how my dad works in

office as his work seems to be completely different

than what mom does. Gosh, I have so much to

learn. The time is passing so slowly". I keep

mumbling to myself.

We had gone to the market on 26th Nov 2017.

That's the second day when mom vomited. During

this stage, especially the first three months, the

senses tend to become stronger and would be moms

get averse to any smell – good or bad. Remember, I

had told that we purchased a new car couple of

months back. Now, every new car has that smell of

leather which takes some months to go. Mom was

waiting in the car as dad had gone to take something

from the shop in the market. I could sense that mom

is uneasy. And then suddenly, she opened the door, went outside and vomited. It is not a pleasing sight to see mom vomiting on the road. *"Mom, please don't worry. Get in. I am fine."* My consoling continues in all the situations. As soon as dad realized, he got a water bottle and we straight away headed home.

Morning sickness is defined when moms during pregnancy vomit or feel dizzy in the morning. My mom was so preoccupied in getting ready for the school and to ensure reaching on time, she hardly had any morning sickness. At her school, all the friendly aunts were advising. *You do not get morning sickness? cool, this is going to be a baby boy. Your tummy is round which predicts a boy again. Your child's heartbeat is 150+, it's a girl.*

Well, only I know who I am, but let the secret continue and time will tell much to the excitement of everyone.

On 2nd Dec 2017, we met the doctor again. *"Everything is going fine"! the doctor said. Keep taking precautions. I have prescribed some additional vitamin and calcium pills, do take them on time. Eat healthy. Moms will advise food, what to eat, what not to eat. But judge yourself and take precaution."* These doctors keep saying this stuff day and day out. They must have memorized the script by now. I wondered.

I am good at counting mom! I was counting the number of times she vomits. 3rd Dec 2017 was the third occasion. I do not know about the future, but I like keeping track of things.

Time was passing by and we were all planning for our Udaipur trip. Exciting, exhausted, but the planning was done. It was decided that we will drive down to Ajmer, stay there overnight and then drive to Udaipur. The plan was ambitious, but my father is an eager driver and willing to go to any place considering that he is driving.

We wanted to be vigilant. 17th Dec 2017, we got a check-up done. To dampen the spirits, the test revealed that I am low lying. This situation is very common when the child is low lying in the belly but comes up eventually. However, lots of rest has to be taken and jerks have to be avoided at all costs. Our doctor clearly stated no to travel. This was disheartening as we were planning for the trip. Dad was so excited about meeting everyone. Even

Grandpa and grandma (Dad's mama mainji) were coming from US for this trip and the enthusiasm levels were very high. *All things happen for good. I sighed. Never mind, I will meet everyone once I am outside. It will be fun to play with everyone and show my tantrums. In this current state, it will be fatiguing for mom only.* So, finally with heavy hearts, we had to say no to the trip at the last moment.

CHAPTER 5 – FOURTH MONTH (24th Dec to 23rd Jan 2018)

December is the holiday period. With Christmas around, the whole city is draped in celebrations. We also went to Ambience mall to celebrate. I do not know the significance of Christmas in detail, but I was reading with my mom. Christmas is celebrated as the birth of Jesus. *I like stories. I can hear stories whole day. It is immensely audible the way mom recites.*

On 28th Dec 2017, grandpa and grandma from US, visited us. They came to spend a day. *Gifts! I love them. Can I open?* I was jumping inside mummy on meeting them and especially the gifts they got. *Tell me more about Ashvika jiji! What does she do, what are her habits, when can I meet her next?* Ashvika jiji is my cousin and she is the cutest child around. *I want to be like her.* I told myself as new adventures of her were unfolded by my grandparents. Whole night, I could not sleep, but was thinking how I will behave and react when I will meet her for the first time. I will be a naughty young sibling, for sure. Next day, Arun nanaji and Anju naniji also came to see me. They had come to drop Diksha mausi at the airport and dropped by to see mummy and papa. *We will play together,* I thought as we ended the day.

With new year around the corner, Neha mausi and Vijay mausaji along with my sister Navya jiji came home. *I am so excited to see you Navya jiji. You are so caring and adorable. We will play together once I come out in this beautiful world.*

We will go to every place together. Mom has great ideas for us and she advises Navya jiji that she will have to take care of this little one. We partied together, ate, sung and celebrated. Mom needs rest and understandably, Neha mausi managed the whole stuff.

2nd January 2017 morning, everything was going fine. My grandma goes for dialysis and she was cleaning the dust when she tripped over the carpet and fell down. There was a loud thud and then lots of cries by grandma. All of us came running outside to witness the tragedy. *I am worried grandma, what happened? Please do not cry and try to get up".* I, so wanted, to help desperately. It was a desperate situation. Mom got really worried. After waiting for couple of hours, the situation did not improve, so grandpa called for an ambulance. *What is happening? Please someone tell me. I was crying as I could not understand the pain and suffering but could only hear the cries of grandma. Please god, help her and get her well soon.* Mom and I stayed back as dad and grandpa went to the hospital. Mom was frantically calling everyone and informing. *Mom tell me, what's happening? My brain and ears are not developed enough to understand these things.* Grandma is a fighter. She has been battling dialysis, blood pressure, diabetes and other couple of diseases, but still maintains a smile on her face. She has expressed multiple times on how she wants to hold me, hug me and kiss me. As the day passed by, doctors informed dad and grandpa that grandma will have to go through a critical surgery and a rod will be placed in her leg. Due to her illness, this can be very dangerous too. With no alternative around, she had to be operated. For next 2 days, my heartbeats were high. I finally relaxed when we got the news that grandma is fine and has been operated successfully. We got her back to home on 7th Jan 2018, but she has been advised 6 months of bed rest. A walker and a wheelchair was arranged at home to make her mobile for her weekly visits for dialysis. *"I promise grandma, when I come out, I will ensure that she is absolutely fine"*.

January is always a stirring month. Dad's birthday falls on 10th January and mom always does something funky. *It's a secret, I know as mom told me.* I kept my little finger on my mouth to keep quiet, as if others can hear me. *"I am going to order a beer cake",* mom told me. It will be a perfect cake for my beer-a-holic dad. I was so happy to be part of the birthday celebration, probably too much, as mom vomited for the 7th time that night. This was more frequent after 3 consecutive sessions on 5th, 6th and 7th January 2018. Tuesday, being a vegetarian day, could not even dampen the spirits. *"Happy Birthday Papa, Many happy returns of the day!"* I wish I could hug him and even tried moving inside mummy. But, the cuddle by my mummy was warm enough to make me happy and feel special to be among the best people.

Our doctor examined mom and me on 20th Jan 2018 and informed that everything is normal. She makes my parents hear the heartbeat every time which runs a smile on their faces. Much to the relaxation of everyone around, the same treatment continued.

CHAPTER 6 – FIFTH MONTH (24th Jan to 23rd Feb 2018)

The fifth month started from 24th Jan 2018 onwards. Time is passing by quickly. I am enjoying inside. Lots of sumptuous food and fruits keeps me occupied throughout the day. My mom's school continued, and I was travelling each day with her. The early morning winter drives are fanciful. There is a bit of fog throughout the route, less traffic and beautiful music played in the car. I heard my parents say multiple times – "this is like a golden period, we three, a small family adoring, singing and driving. I like driving. Multiple times, I stirred from left side to right side inside my mom's abdomen to get closer to dad and see how he drives. Mom even felt the movement and informed dad too.

"Why there are so many buttons papa?" I wish to press them to see what happens, but my hands are still developing. *"Once I come out, will you let me play with all of these?"* I enquired. With the satisfaction that I will not be denied, I felt happy and continued to enjoy the rides to school.

At the same time, the medical tests continued for my mom. The list seemed to be infinite:

1. Anti Rubella IGG

2. Anti Rubella IGM

3. CBC

4. FBS – Glucose (Fasting)

5. HBSAG

6. TSH

7. VDRL (RPR/Syphilis)

8. Blood Group ABO

9. Urine analysis

10. HB Electrophoresis

11. HIV

12. HCV

13. Total Beta HCG

14. USG

She was also asked to take medicines regularly

1. Sysfol active – one tablet once a day

2. Susten SR – one tablet once a day

3. Doxinate – one tablet twice a day

"Phew"! So many tests. I am a little fellow and these tests seem to be some alphabets for me. I want to learn ABCD, but these are difficult. Best of luck mom." I was always conscious during these tests and kept enquiring mom, *"are you ok? Can't you tell these people that I am saying I am alright*

here. I am enjoying, and these tests worry me more than anything else.".

Anyhow, doctor knows best and our doctor is the best. Mom keeps saying this to dad and as an biddable child, I observe and say yes too.

3rd Feb 2018 is an interesting day. This would be the first day when my parents will see me. *"Whoohoo"*! I am excited. Doctor will conduct the ultrasound. This is a more advanced ultrasound where she will make my parents see the limbs.

"Ok"! So, it is time for me to show some more tantrums. When the test started, the doctor was able to observe me. But for checking my spine, I had to turn around. *"So here is my chance".* I will not turn around. The doctor kept pressing mom here and there, it felt as someone is tickling me, but I did not budge. Finally, the doctor gave up and asked my mom to have some water and coffee and then come back. *"the little champ might turn then"*, doctor said with a low tone. *"Ha ha ha ha"*, I giggled. My little competitive spirit won. *"Go on mom, have coffee. I like coffee. Please ask for extra sugar. I have a sweet tooth."* Mom understands my feelings. She exactly had coffee with extra sugar. Now, with such sweetness, how can I remain stubborn. I turned and showed my spine to the doctor.

So, here the sequence goes.

1. My head – *"Is it like dad or mom?"*

2. My neck – *"I am going to be like mom here. Let's see what mom and dad think"*.

3. Face – My parents were able to spot the nasal bone

4. Spine – So, this is the one for which we had a scrumptious coffee

5. Chest – *"I am going to be like dad"*

6. Abdomen – *"Foodie is going to be my second name"*

7. Limbs – All normal

So, all is normal with me that brought smile to everyone around. Doctor also checked for Down Syndrome, but nothing can affect me. I have affectionate family and I will kick all such things out of the system.

I am just 18MM big, so clear pictures are not possible and not permissible by law also. I am really surprised why is there such a need for this kind of law. My parents never talked about whether they want a girl or a boy. They thought about the names for both, dresses etc and never once even thought about it. I wonder everyone can be like this, so that will be so good. Anyhow, I continue to ponder over my good luck.

The most exciting was to see my hand and my toes. *"That's it parents. Slowly and steady".* The doctor counted the fingers – 1, 2, 3, 4…….10. *"I can count, I can count. Let me do it again. Baan, tu, thee, phol….. ten".* I counted again with my parents.

The month continued with regular jobs. On 12th Feb again, mom had to go for a regular check-up. What got added to mom's diet was Baby & Me health drink. Dad was excited to get it instantaneously and made sure that he got up every morning to make mom drink with milk.

My movements are growing. Every now and then, I would show sign of movements and mom would immediately show it to dad.

CHAPTER 7 – SIXTH MONTH (24th Feb to 23rd Mar 2018)

Late February is the time when winter verdures India, but it leaves behind cough and cold. This change of season invariably impacts everyone and so did to mom. For 5 continuous days, she has been coughing. On 5th Mar 2018, we had an appointment with the doctor as part of the regular check-up. There was a tension as this should not be impacting me inside.

"I am ok. There is a protection around me. Nothing gets inside here except the deliciuous food. This is enjoyment at its fullest." But, this is not known to my parents. Doctor explained the same thing which provided comfort. Same medicines continued for mom.

CBC was counseled. Mom has gotten used to the tests so much that needle pricking does not matter her at all.

This is the month of holi. Mom does not like colors, but I feel it is really an entertaining festival. I got to know about it when we got the invitation from mom's uncle. Mom is apple of everyone's eyes in the family and she was bound to get special attention during this special time. It is a 45-minute drive from our place. But, we took almost 90 minutes. Thanks to dad trying to avoid all the potholes and bad traffic. We snarled through at an average speed of around 20 kmph. *"Common dad! Speed up. I want to meet the whole family."* Finally we reached, the lasts one to reach, and I was not happy about it. But, everyone greeted us and asked about me. It felt that I am like a superstar. *"I am doing great, thank you everyone"!* I exclaimed. Mom got the best seat in the living room and all the food was served to her.

Holi is a festival of colors. I am going to play with all the colors available once I grow up. Will put colors on everyone. I was enjoying seeing others play holi. Mom and mainji placed themselves in the balcony away from others. Dad was extra protective and asked to put colors on him instead of mom. The day ended enjoying, chatting and laughing.

My parents anniversary falls on 21st February. They have had exploratory anniversaries always, like couple of day's visit to Jaipur, a balloon safari on the other. This time, since they had a tiny little fellow with them, who is yet to reconnoiter the world, the celebrations were restricted to a family dinner. *"We will go to balloon safari Mumma, papa!"* I was excited as both my parents discussed and looked at the pictures of balloon safari. I need to be 4 feet tall in order to be allowed, *"I will gain height quickly"*. Thinking about it, I slept along with mom, with the world's best safety and comfort, on our return from dinner.

7th March 2019, we got the results of the various tests. Mom went through CBC. All the results were positive except iron. Iron deficiency was identified and from there on, the advices again started pouring in. Mom followed each and started eating Gooseberry and Spinach and it really worked well. She was determined not to get herself injected with iron injections, so a natural way was adopted.

We are glad that we live in a world where medicine is so advanced. I am not sure what I want to become on growing, but the world seems fascinating. *"When will these 9 months be over"?*

CHAPTER 7 – SEVENTH MONTH (24th Mar to 23rd Apr 2018)

We enter the 7th month. The excitement is growing to see the world around. I am growing fast. Mom's vomit sessions continue. *"Eiu, mom!*

Can you please control?" But , apparently, this happens and I believe it takes out all the bad things from mom's stomach and keeps it clean for me.

The tests continue to take place. Our doctor, a perfect gynae, never took chance and asked my mom to keep going through tests.

- Glucose Fasting

- Glucose 60 min.

- Glucose 120 min.

- CBC

- Urine analysis

- Hemoglobin

- Chemical Examination

- Microscopic Examination

Her medication continued too

- Orofer

- Limcee

- Supracal

- Looz Syrup

- And many more

Mom follows the diet strictly. She always does what she commits too. Much like Salman Khan – *"Ek baar jo maine commitment kar di, phir mein apni bhi nahi suntan".* Similarly, she committed herself to green veggies and did not touch Maida, fried products and fruits like Papaya during the whole pregnancy. No matter how much my father kept enjoying these things. *"mom, we will go out and eat all these things. I will be a foodie".* Things don't turn out as planned always. When we showed mom's reports to the doctor, she advised that there is iron deficiency. Well, we wanted to avoid unnecessary medicine and from then on,

spinach was a daily staple for mom.

All this while, regular life continues. Dad will drive

the car to his office. From there, mom would take

over and carefully drive to her school. I loved these

drives. Early mornings, no traffic, good music and

coziness and safety of my parents. Moreover, I

don't have to get up and get ready like others. I am

relaxed in my own little beautiful dark world.

CHAPTER 8 –EIGHT MONTH
(24th Apr to 23rd May 2018)

There were daily phone calls and weekend visits from relatives. From all the conversations, I realized that my dad's side of relatives are all outside – In USA and Canada. My Dadi are 3 siblings. That's exciting. *"When are we visiting them or they visiting us dad? Let me see if I can name everyone (Papa told me though)"*

- USA wale Babaji

- USA wali Dadi

- Ashu Tauji

- Devika Taiji

- Malu bhua (Dad's excited about your marriage and plans are being formed.

- Ashvika Jiji (Huggy Puggy Jiji)

- Canada wale Babaji

- Canada wali Dadi

- Lavanya Bhua

- Gulnar Bhua

Yippee, I should be seeing them all. Ok, so this was papa's side. My mom's side is a huge family and most of them live in Delhi NCR. My Nani are 5 sisters, so let me see if I can name all my Nanis and their families -

- Nani

- Neha Mausi

- Mausajiji (For me Jiji will be one word, so it becomes Mausajiji, isn't it? I am nifty)

- Navya Jiji (She is going to be our kids leader)

- Lawrence Road wale Nana

- Achint Mama
- Neeti mainji
- Kushagra Dada
- Sulabh Mama
- Nidhi Mainji
- Deepu Nani
- Deepu Nani Nana
- Shikha Mausi
- Rachit Mausaji
- Ashvi Jiji
- Risha Jiji
- Ankit Mama
- Ankita Mainji
- Ansh
- Charu Nani

- Charu Nani Nana

- Praguni Mausi

- Ankit Mausaji

- Reyansh Dada

- Shubhra Mausi

- Anju Nani (Well, I will end up calling her Andu Nani, egg will be my favorite dish)

- Anju Nani Nana

- Diksha Mausi

- Akshata Mausi

My Nana are also 4 siblings and the families are spread in India, Hong Kong, USA and Australia

- Nana

- Bade Nana

- Sonu Mama

- Mainji

- Priyanshi Jiji (She is going to be caring and will be on my side instead of Rudr Dada always)

- Rudr Dada (We will have the most fun when I will be in Ajmer or you in Delhi)

- Dolly Nani

- Australia wali Nani

- Australia wale Nana

- Rashmi Mausi

- Vidit Mausaji

- Vihaan dada

- Aiyana jiji

- Mallika Mausi

- Haren Mausaji

- Jaya jiji

<u>CHAPTER 9 – NINTH MONTH</u>
(24th May to 23rd Jun 2018)

It could be any day. My arrival to this stunning world. Like anyone else, I had my plans. The immediate one was that I am not going to trouble mom during the delivery. It all started when I began pushing and kicking. By now, my kicks and movements were discernable. *"I am growing big mom, need some space, sorry!"* I was apologetic but knew that no one is going to mind these tantrums.

We had our dinner. Since nana and nani are here, the food had to be delicious with wide variety. Having them around is always a bolstering factor. Mom started complaining of disquiet since 11pm. Since it was usual during these days, everyone advised her to take rest and sleep. The pain started after a while. *"Mom, I need to come out. There's no space left."* I was kicking hard. It could be seen from outside. Pushing with my tiny little hands and feet. *"How can they take it easy? It is a nighttime and as a cunning little kid, I had to trouble them in the night only."* What fun if it's a daytime.

At 0130 hours, it all started. Boy! Mom burst her water bag. Dad who was half asleep, did not know what to do. Poor guy, he asked mom what next and got the scolding of his lifetime. *"call mom and take me to hospital, right now"*. Mom exclaimed.

The hospital, Venkateshwara Hospital in Dwarka, is a 20 min drive from our home. Quickly everyone got ready. Nani helped Mom to wear loose clothes and, in the meantime, dad got the car. Since it was urgent, mom, dad, nana and nani, we all rushed to the hospital. Dada and Dadi locked the house and then they also rushed to the hospital. My grandfather usually doesn't drive at night, but he there was no second thought on that night.

"This is exciting"! I will be able to see the stunning world. I will be able to materially meet all those people who took care of me, wished well for me and who will be playing an imperative role in my wellbeing. The ride to hospital was fun. We never noticed the speed breakers, red lights or the potholes earlier, but that night, my mom made dad feel that he is the worst driver ever to be born.

Finally, we reached the hospital. A grand hospital with all the modern facilities available. It was selected by my parents after scrutiny and erudition about the doctors. Eventually, the research was going to be paid off soon.

It was 4am when mom was admitted. The nurses were very supportive. They calmed my Nani and mom. After all the formalities were done, mom was taken inside the labour room. *"What do I need to do? How do I make sure my mom doesn't undergo a lot of pain? Can you tell me?"* My feeble voice was shouting at top of its voice, but aghast, no one can hear me. *"Let me come out, I am going to cry on top of my voice that the nursing staff will certainly make note of it".* I stated to myself. With every passing nurse, I tried to talk. *"This is my first-time sister, can anyone tell me what do I need to do?"*

The doctor was informed, but as always it happens, you don't get what you hoped for. Since the delivery date was 6th July, but here we were in the hospital on 20th June 2018, my doctor had gone out for vacation. So, we were entirely in the hands of another doctor. *"Hmm, now this is a challenge. How would a new doctor know the history?"* I tried to reason, but these days medical and technology is so advanced that you don't have to care for these things. It was 8 o'clock when the doctor came out and stated that all is ok, but my mom has to be inserted pain so that normal delivery can be done. All my family wanted a normal delivery. I too. *"Why should mom go through the caesarean when her child wants to co-operate, and everything is fine?"* I so badly wanted to let everyone know but felt destitute. Doctor also informed that it will take 4-5 hours for the delivery to be done, so everyone can go back home, get ready and come back. It made sense since no one had slept last night and did not have anything in breakfast.

A decision was made that my father will stay, and others can go home, get ready, have breakfast and come back refreshed to welcome me.

9am, the preparations were done to take my mom to the delivery room. Dad was called in and was allowed to meet mom as she was driven away to the delivery room. She was shouting and crying in pain and held my dad's hand to do something. The last few hours have been tough on him. Not knowing what needs to be done, he was just flowing with emotions and went on what was advised without questions. The last thing my mother could have expected was a smile with no comforting words and that's what he gave her. He smiled and said everything is going to be fine. Imagine, you in a lot of pain and the only person whom you can talk to you, smiles rather than being empathetic, will make you mad with anger. But I was enjoying. I was jumping with bliss, not knowing that it is causing more pain to mom.

After multiple attempts, I slipped out at 9.45am. Proving all predictions that it will take 4-5 hours, wrong. The petite life was out there much to the delight of everyone around. *"BRING IT ON"!* I said. *"I am here and I am fine".* The medical staff understood who I wanted to see first and that's what they did. They took me and placed my little body on top of my mother's abdominal. She was exhausted in pain and did not know how to react. Whether she should cry in pain or beam in seeing someone whom she nurtured for 9 months inside her and will be providing utmost attention and love for rest of her life. I could sense confusion on seeing a pale purple little life. But mind you, I am smart and I am handsome and over a period of time will be fair too.

That meeting was interrupted as mom had to be taken away for dressing and I had to be geared up too. On the way, they called dad to come over and meet the child. Assuming that it will take 4-5 hours, my father went to the main corridor to charge the phone. That was smart as it was the only means of communication available to him at that time, but dad, how can you not think that your kid is going to be smarted and will slip out to prove everyone wrong. The guard had to run all the way to the corridor to inform me. Dad was thrilled. Not knowing what to do with the charger and phone, he left both things up there for anyone's grab and reached the labour room. Medical staff showed me to him. That is one moment, I cannot forget. We both looked at each other, eye to eye for the first time and I could see twinkle in his eye. 30 seconds passed as if they were only a second. My father finally asked, is it a boy or a girl? Since the medical staff cannot reveal the gender until they hand over the baby, they pulled the linen that covered me and asked – "see for yourself". *"That is so rude. I also have a privacy".* I started to cry so much that they had to put the linen back and take me away.

Thrilled, dad came back to the corridor and called up my grandfather. *"IT's A BOY"*. That's it. Probably the shortest phone call he ever made, but I knew that he would never show his other side to anyone, which was jumping up and down in a crowded hospital with tears of happiness on his face.

But after 10 or 15 minutes, panic set in. Dad called my grandfather again and said that he is now not sure whether it's a boy or a girl. Ostensibly, he did not pay attention. It was too late as the news had spread all across in 5 minutes like a bushfire. That would have been embarrassing to inform everyone that, no its not a boy, it's a girl. Silly dad.

He rushed back to the labour room and enquired that can be confirmed what the gender is now. To his respite, they confirmed. With that drama, some more time passed and my grandparent reached hospital. Full of excitement, they all waited for the doctors briefing. Dad was called inside and he was informed that everything is fine with the baby. He is fit, weight is 2.7kg which is normal and more importantly, he need not be diagnosed with a treatment for jaundice which is very common these days. To everyone's surprise, after all the examinations, I made it to our single room in the hospital much before mom was transferred. The hospital room was decorated in my welcome. With balloons and decorations on the door, there were lots of decoration, cake and a photographer present to take those personal pictures of welcoming me and the cuddles. My Aunt, Uncle and Navya jiji also made it to the hospital. *"This is my lovely family. I wanted to meet each of you".* I wanted to say, but my speech and voice will take some time to be developed and recognized. There were non-stop phone calls, messages and wishes from everywhere. The celebrations went on for few hours.

Since this is my autobiography, how can I move ahead without describing me? So here it is. *"I am born with thick black hair. I have a beautiful round face. Big eyes that want to see and understand everything that they see. Long eye lashes that just add to the gorgeous eyes. Cute little nose with sweet pink lips. I am chubby but that's my cuteness, eventually I will make sure I have a well toned muscular body. My hands are tiny ones looking to grab and understand things around. My small legs are always on a move as I want to walk, run and play around. I am tough and do not believe in crying much, but you better agree with me, otherwise I can lift the whole house on my head by crying on top of my voice. My stout cheeks are an attraction for everyone to kiss me. Please, I prefer dry kisses. I am a perfect combination of my parents. With hair, eyes and nose like my mom, face cut, chin, cheeks and other features resemble dad. I don't know what I will become after growing, but so far I am ready to enjoy what is in store for me."*

We stayed in the hospital for 2 days. Dad completed all the formalities. I had to be registered online. Finally, I came to know that mom and dad had already thought a name. Even grandparents agreed to that. *"Ok, common, tell me. What's my name? Some Bollywood superstar as my looks are stunning or a famous sportsperson? Hurry up, tell me?"* My inquisitiveness was ever rising. Then my name was called out.

"MAAHIR MATHUR" born on 20th June 2018

"Wow! That's unique. Mumma, papa, what does it mean?" My vocabulary will take time to develop. *"Maahir means skilled/skilful"*. Mom stated as if she understood my question. A smile appeared on everyone's face, not sure whether they saw it on my face it or not, but I adored the name.

We came home after 2 days. Aunt and Navya jiji had already decorated the house. They had done all the purchasing of necessary items that are required for a new born baby. All the toys were arranged. The cupboards bear the cut outs of bottles, diapers, new born baby essentials and the whole house was adorned. The excitement continued and everyone was loving it. Lot of relatives came to see me. Doctor said that the baby will need 16-18 hours of sleep and breast feeding possibly every 2 hours. Like an obedient boy, I followed that and met everyone in my sleep mostly. Mom was supposed to take rest for at least 2 weeks, so I and mom remained together. Malu bhua was getting married on 14th July 2018 and there were plans for at least dad to attend it. He had promised her.

With every passing day, I was having milk, but vomiting. Perhaps, this is normal. My parents and grandparents casually consulted the doctor and got a reply that this happens. This continued for 14 days and I constantly vomited. I knew something is not right. *"Mom, dad! Something's not right. Please hear me. I feel the milk is not getting digested. I am not able to have it". Dad, dadi, Nana, nani, can you please hear me? SOMETHING's NOT RIGHT".*

<u>CHAPTER 10 – THE SURGERY</u>

"Something's not right! I knew, but not able to communicate. I was taken to the hospital 3 times, but everything seemed normal to the doctors. In our 4th visit within 14 days of my birth, few tests were prescribed. My doctor is a very experienced one. Although he accepted the my initial ultrasound report, he suspected something and asked to get the tests done again.

To everyone's horror, I was diagnosed with Pyloric Stenosis. *"What is that? I can't even pronounce it". What has happened to me?"* I kept weeping and looking for answer, but no one knew exactly.

Pyloric stenosis is a narrowing of the opening from the stomach to the first part of the small intestine (the pylorus). Symptoms include projectile vomiting without the presence of bile. This most often occurs after the baby is fed.   The typical age that symptoms become obvious is two to twelve weeks old. It happens mostly to the first born male child and without surgery the child can even die.

There were tears all over on everyone's face when dad told about his briefing with the doctor to everyone. *"How is that possible, we took the utmost care of the baby. He was born fine, so what is all this non-sense?"* Mom asked surprised and crying.

"Surgery?" I was shocked. *"What are they going to do to me dad, mom? I don't want to go anywhere. I want to be with you."* I was horrified. *"What's happening to me?"* I was looking for answers and so do others around me.

Finally, the procedure was explained. There will be insertion on my abdomen, the surgeon will reach to the intestines and open the partially blocked passage before the small intestine.

A surgery requiring 2 hours on a 14 day old baby! Dad, Baba and Nana approached the doctor in a very well reputed hospital for a second opinion, but the result was same. The baby must be operated.

I was crying non-stop. First, I was becoming weak due to constant vomiting. Then I need to undergo a surgery and finally, it seems that I will be away from my family for few days, when I needed them the most.

Dr. Mehendiratta and Dr Anjani are the most experienced doctors around for these kinds of cases and they were supposed to operate on me. *"Will I be fine doctor? Please take care of me. I am a little fellow, can't even express myself. I want to be with my parents. I want to grow big and strong.*

I will be a good boy always. Promise." I said nervously, knowing that my language is unknown to this world.

Finally, with the consent of my parents, thee day and date was decided. I had to be kept in observation and there was constant beating on my back by nurses so that some milk can stay inside or I can digest most of it. *"It hurts, please don't do that. I want to be with my mom. Please take me to her."* It was a agony for my mom too, whose stitches were not even healed and she had to stay for a week in the hospital. I had to be fed every 3 hours and that's why my parents were asked to stay in the waiting room. No matter how comfortable the sofa cum bed were there, their comfort lied with me only. Every night dad used to get a wheel chair for mom to carry her to the Nursery so that she could feed me. Such a strong lady my mom is that never once she thought about herself. She bore all pain but made sure I stay healthy only by being fed with mother's milk. Only she knows what was in her mind seeing her baby away from her, on the verge of being surgically operated and vomiting every single time she is feeding him. I cried and cried and cried, much due to hunger, due to being away from my mom and seeing the circumstances that they were going through.

"I am sorry mom. This is not my intention. I am not like this. Once I will be fine, I will never leave you and will always cuddle around you." I was positive. *"Can please someone convey my message to her?"* The restlessness was obvious.

The surgery went well. But, the misery had to continue. I was diagnosed with jaundice due to lack of mother's milk in the past 4 days. So, an ordeal of another 2 days had began with me being operated for jaundice. Although, this was not severe and I could hear doctors talk that I will be fine, I shifted my focus to things around. There were 6 kids including me in the room where we were operated for jaundice. There was a girl to me left and a boy to my right. To my surprise, mom always found me tilted towards left always. It was never intentional but perhaps I am left-handed like my dad, you know.

We were discharged on 12th July much to the happiness of everyone around. Dad was sad as he could not attend bhua's marriage. *"Please do not blame him Malu bhua, I am the felon. I will make up for all the lost time when we will meet"*. I prayed for her happy married life and went back to see how the celebrations again began.

Now, I am feeding well, not leaving mom for a split second. I sleep on her, I hug her and want to spend joyful times with the family.

"Thank you everyone for patiently reading my journey. I wanted to share it as it was special. I am born as human which is a gift in itself and would like to contribute towards the human race to justify

www.ingramcontent.com/pod-product-compliance
Lightning Source LLC
Chambersburg PA
CBHW020625160726
47991CB00002BA/931